The Snowman™

RAYMOND BRIGGS

HAMISH HAMILTON

London

Other books by Raymond Briggs
THE MOTHER GOOSE TREASURY
THE FAIRY TALE TREASURY
*
THE ELEPHANT AND THE BAD BABY *text by Elfrida Vipont*
JIM AND THE BEANSTALK
*
FATHER CHRISTMAS
FATHER CHRISTMAS GOES ON HOLIDAY
FUNGUS THE BOGEYMAN
GENTLEMAN JIM
THE FUNGUS THE BOGEYMAN PLOP-UP BOOK
WHEN THE WIND BLOWS
THE TIN-POT FOREIGN GENERAL AND THE OLD IRON WOMAN
UNLUCKY WALLY
UNLUCKY WALLY TWENTY YEARS ON

HAMISH HAMILTON CHILDREN'S BOOKS
Published by the Penguin Group
27 Wrights Lane, London W8 5TZ, England
Viking Penguin Inc., 40 West 23rd Street, New York, New York 10010, USA
Penguin Books Australia Ltd, Ringwood, Victoria, Australia
Penguin Books Canada Ltd, 2801 John Street, Markham, Ontario, Canada L3R 1B4
Penguin Books (NZ) Ltd, 182-190 Wairau Road, Auckland 10, New Zealand

Penguin Books Ltd, Registered Offices: Harmondsworth, Middlesex, England

First published in Great Britain 1978 by
Hamish Hamilton Children's Books

Copyright © 1978 by Raymond Briggs

9 10

ISBN 0-241-10004-6

British Library Cataloguing in Publication Data
is available from the British Library

Printed and bound in Italy by Printer Trento s.r.l.

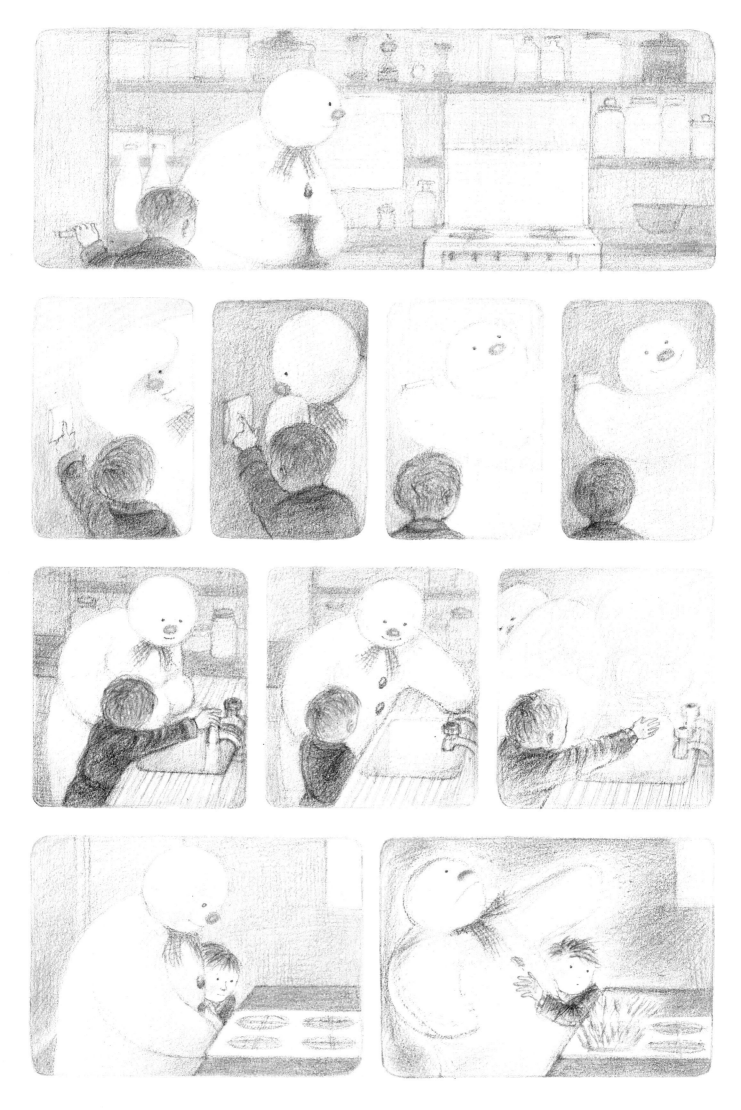